The Bailey School Kids Joke Book

by Daniella Burr

based on books by
Debbie Dadey and Marcia Thornton Jones

illustrated by John Steven Gurney

A
LITTLE APPLE
PAPERBACK

SCHOLASTIC INC.
New York Toronto London Auckland Sydney

No part of this publication may be reproduced in whole or in part, or stored in a retrieval system, or transmitted in any form or by any means, electronic, mechanical, photocopying, recording, or otherwise, without written permission of the publisher. For information regarding permission, write to Scholastic Inc., 555 Broadway, New York, NY 10012.

ISBN 0-590-99552-9

12 11 10 9 8 7   7 8 9/9 0 1/0

Printed in the U.S.A.   40

First Scholastic printing, September 1996

Book design by Laurie Williams

Welcome to Bailey School!

Eddie, Melody, Howie, and Liza are in Mrs. Jeepers' third-grade class. Most of the kids at Bailey School think that Mrs. Jeepers is a vampire! When she gets mad, her green eyes flash and she rubs her mysterious green brooch.

There are lots of other *strange* grown-ups living in Bailey City. Here are some wacky jokes from those wacky folks!

A collection of Mrs. Jeepers' favorite Transylvanian ticklers!

Mrs. Jeepers *from*
VAMPIRES DON'T WEAR POLKA DOTS

Liza: How can you tell if a vampire has a cold?
Nurse Smedley: He starts coffin'!

Eddie: What is a vampire's favorite holiday?
Melody: Fangs-giving!

Howie: Why did the vampire cross the road?
Mr. Drake: To bite someone on the other side!

Why did the vampire go to the orthodontist?
To improve his bite!

1

Liza: What is Dracula's favorite treat?
Huey: An all-day sucker!

Carey: What is the best way to phone a
vampire?
Melody: Long distance!

What does a vampire with good man-
ners say to his victim?
It's been really nice gnawing you.

Eddie: Why did the vampires cancel
their softball game?
Coach Snarley: They couldn't find their
bats.

What did the vampire say when he
called the blood bank?
Do you deliver?

Liza: What is Count Dracula's favorite
sport?
Coach Graves: Skin diving!

2

Ben: What kind of coat does a vampire
wear on a rainy day?
Melody: A wet one!

How do you stop the pain of vampire
bites?
Don't bite any!

Liza: When does Dracula find time to
eat?
Mrs Jeepers: During his coffin break!

Eddie: What is a vampire's favorite meal?

Mrs. Tilly: Ghoul-ash!

How does one vampire greet another vampire?

Hello, sucker!

Eddie: Why don't vampires eat T-bones and sirloins?

Howie: Because they stay away from stakes!

What goes flap flap chomp chomp ouch?

A vampire with a toothache!

Mr. Jenkins' werewolf jokes will make you howl!

Mr. Jenkins *from*
WEREWOLVES DON'T GO TO SUMMER CAMP

Why shouldn't you invite werewolves to your house?
They'll shed on your couch!

Why did it take the werewolf three days to finish a ten page book?
He wasn't very hungry.

What kind of fur do you get from a werewolf?
As fur away as you can get!

What are two things a werewolf can't have for breakfast?
Lunch and supper.

What would you get if you crossed peanut butter, bread, jelly, and a werewolf?

A hairy peanut butter sandwich that howls when the moon is full!

What kind of snack does a werewolf eat?

Lady fingers!

Knock-knock.
Who's there?
Howl.
Howl who?
Howl we know if the werewolf is coming?

Which side of a werewolf has the most fur?

The outside!

Where was the werewolf when the lights went out?

In the dark!

Knock-knock.
Who's there?
Phil.
Phil who?
Phil my face. Is it getting hairy?

Who is a werewolf's favorite old-time movie star?
Scary Grant!

What do werewolves eat to celebrate October 31?
Hallo-weenies.

Why does the werewolf eat raw meat?
He doesn't know how to cook.

What would you get if you crossed a werewolf with a parrot?
I don't know, but you'd better give him a cracker when he asks for it!

Mr. Merlin is a whiz on the library's computer! Here are some jokes with byte!

Mr. Merle *from*
WIZARDS DON'T NEED COMPUTERS

Howie: What goes snap, crackle, pop?
Liza: A computer with a short circuit.

Melody: What do you get when you cross a computer with an elephant?
Carey: A five-ton know-it-all!

Ben: I think I'd like to be a space computer engineer.
Eddie: That would be the perfect job for you. After all, you take up space at Bailey School!

Mr. Merle: Did you hear about the computer that swallowed a yo-yo?

Melody: Yes. It gave the same answer ten times!

Liza: Why did the computer whiz bring a computer to school?

Eddie: Her mother told her to give an Apple to the teacher!

A cauldron of wacky witch jokes!

Miss Brewbaker *from*
WITCHES DON'T DO BACKFLIPS

What happened to the little witches
who ate all of their vegetables?
They gruesome.

Why do witches go around scaring
people?
They're just trying to eek out a living!

Why do witches ride brooms?
Vacuum cleaners make too much noise.

What is a baby witch's favorite fairy
tale?
Ghoul-dilocks and the Three Brrrs.

Why did the witch go on a diet?
To keep her ghoulish figure!

Where does a witch keep her wallet?
In her hag bag.

How did the witch get around after her broom broke?
She witch-hiked!

Did you hear about the dog trainer who learned how to cast spells?
He went from wags to witches!

How do you make a witch scratch?
Take away the W.

What do you get if you cross a witch with a mummy?
A flying Band-Aid!

Why do witches wear pointed black hats?
To keep their heads warm!

What happened to the witch's black cat when he ate a lemon?
He became a sour puss!

What did the teenage witch ask her mom?
Can I have the keys to the broom tonight?

What desserts do witches order in Chinese restaurants?
Mis-fortune cookies!

Where do witches go to get their hair done?
To the boo-ty parlor!

Did you hear about the bad luck witch?
When a black cat crossed her path the cat got bad luck!

Mr. Jolly has a sackful of holiday ho-hos for you!

Mr. Jolly *from*
SANTA CLAUS DOESN'T MOP FLOORS

Where does Santa dry his suit?
On a Claus line!

What happens if you eat Christmas tree trimmings?
You get tinsil-itis!

What is green and sour and gives presents at Christmas?
Santa Pickle!

What does Tarzan sing at Christmastime?
Jungle Bells!

What goes "Ho ho ho *SWOOSH*"?
Santa Claus caught in a revolving door!

Knock-knock.
Who's there?
Claus.
Claus who?
Quick, claus the door! It's freezing in here!

Howie: Did you hear about the pig who began hiding garbage in November?
Melody: She wanted to do her Christmas slopping early!

Mr. Cooper's Best Books from the Bailey City Library

Every book's a laugh and a half!

The Final Bell
by Gladys Saturday

Mousetrap!
by Chet R. Cheese

The Long Walk to School
by Misty Buss

All New Practical Jokes
by Major Crack-up

I Can't See the Screen
by Sid Down

A Week at the Shore
by Fay Cation

Entering the Haunted House
by Hugo First

On the Ocean Floor
by Sandy Bottoms

Working for Peanuts
by Ella Funt

The Complete Guide to Hopscotch
by Rhea Cess

A Career in Gasoline
by Phil R. Upp

I Love Algebra
by Just Joe King

Mr. Drake's Transylvanian Top Ten

Mr. Drake *from*
DRACULA DOESN'T DRINK LEMONADE

1. Dracula's Favorite Coffee:
   De-coffin-ated

2. Dracula's Favorite Snack: Fangfurters

3. Dracula's Favorite Animal: Giraffe

4. Dracula's Favorite Cook:
   Batty Crocker

5. Dracula's Favorite Fruit: Necktarines

6. Dracula's Favorite Disease:
   High Blood Pressure

7. Dracula's Favorite City: Veinice, Italy

8. Dracula's Favorite Eye Color:
   Blood Shot

9. Dracula's Favorite Ice Cream:
   Toothy Fruity

10. Dracula's Favorite Song:
    Fangs for the Memories

Goofy bus rides that will drive you crazy!

Mr. Stone *from*
GARGOYLES DON'T DRIVE SCHOOL BUSES

Melody: Why don't you take the bus home?
Huey: My mother will only make me bring it back again!

Liza: Who can hold up a school bus with only one hand?
Carey: A policeman!

Howie: What happened to you when you missed the bus?
Eddie: I caught it when I got home!

Liza: Why did they bury the school bus?
Melody: The engine died.

Hearty hamburger ha-has!

Mrs. Rosenbloom *from*
CUPID DOESN'T FLIP HAMBURGERS

Liza: Yuck! There's a bug in my french fries.
Eddie: Don't worry. The spider on your hamburger will eat it in no time!

Where do the outstanding hamburgers wind up?
In the Hall of Flame!

Where do burgers dance?
At a meatball!

Where do hamburgers box?
In an onion ring!

Why did Huey climb to the top of the fast food restaurant?
He heard the burgers were on the house!

Why does everyone get together at the hamburger joint?
It's a great place to meat!

Eddie: Why are you blowing so hard on your hamburger?
Liza: It's better than eating it.

Howie: Yuck! There's a spider on my hamburger.
Mrs. Rosenbloom: Of course there is. It's the fly's day off.

Knock-knock.
Who's there?
Howard.
Howard who?
Howard you like half of my hamburger?

What did the cheeseburger say to the pickle?
You're dill-licious!

Where is the best place to taste a hamburger?
In your mouth.

These jokes are so funny they'll wake the undead!

Coach Graves *from*
ZOMBIES DON'T PLAY SOCCER

What happens when zombies laugh?
They make ghouls of themselves!

What is dead, creepy, and has a red nose?
Rudolph the red-nosed zombie!

What can't you sell to a zombie?
Life insurance!

What kinds of books do zombies love?
Books with a cemetery plot!

Where will you find a sleeping zombie?
In the dead room!

What is the difference between zombies and torn socks?

Zombies are dead men, torn socks are mended.

Eddie: Did you hear the one about the zombie's grave?

Ben: No.

Eddie: Oh, never mind. You wouldn't dig it.

Liza: What do you call a zombie that rides coach class on an airplane?

Howie: A passenger.

No bones about it — these jokes are funny!

Mr. Belgrave *from*
SKELETONS DON'T PLAY TUBAS

Why didn't the skeleton go to the movies?
It had no body to go with!

What kind of crew sails a haunted ship?
A skeleton crew!

How do skeletons get their mail?
By bony express!

What is a skeleton's favorite instrument?
The trom-bone!

Why is a skeleton like a sea treasure?
It has a sunken chest!

How do you make a skeleton laugh?
Tickle his funny bone

What do you get when you cross a
skeleton with peanut butter?
Extra-crunchy peanut butter!

How does one skeleton talk to another?
On the tele-bone!

Why wasn't the skeleton afraid of the
police?
*He knew they couldn't pin anything on
him!*

Why don't skeletons fight each other?
They don't have the guts!

Why did the skeleton go to the beach?
To get a skele-tan!

If you were walking down the street
and you saw two skeletons, a werewolf,
and a vampire, what should you do?
Hope it's Halloween!

Mr. Belgrave's Musical Jokes

Take 🎵*: The laughs are on their way!*

Liza: What did the tuba call his
father?
Howie: Oom Papa.

Why is nothing better than a broken
drum?
Because you can't beat it!

Mrs. Jeepers: How long is the song
"Soap, Soap, Soap, Soap"?
Eddie: Four bars!

Melody: What kind of band doesn't
make music?
Mr. Davis: A rubber band!

Huey: What do you get if you fall on
a CD?
Carey: A slipped disk!

What is a frying pan's favorite song?
Home on the Range!

Eddie: Why do teakettles whistle?
Aunt Mathilda: Because they never
learned how to sing!

What do you get when you cross a
chicken with a guitar?
*A chicken that makes music when
you pluck it!*

Why did the boy put his head on the
piano?
He was trying to play by ear.

What is a cucumber's favorite instrument?
The pickle-o.

Carey: What soft, sweet, chocolate
dessert makes music?
Mrs. Tilly: Cello Pudding!

Howie: What kind of dog plays in orchestras?

Melody: *A trum-pet!*

Green and goofy jokes!

Mr. O'Grady *from*
LEPRECHAUNS DON'T PLAY BASKETBALL

Why did the pigs paint their hooves green?
It was Saint Patrick's Day!

What is green, saves lives, and flies?
Super Leprechaun!

Why did the leprechaun cross the road?
Because the light was green.

What is round, green, and circles the sun?
The planet of the grapes!

A ghoulish group of gags!

Uncle Jasper *from*
GHOSTS DON'T EAT POTATO CHIPS

How is an adult different from a ghost?
One is all grown. The other is all groan.

What do you call a cut on a ghost?
A boo-boo.

What did the mommy ghost say to her son?
Don't spook until you are spooken to!

Where did the lady ghost teach?
At an all-ghoul school!

What do you get when you cross a ghost with a chicken?
A bird that plays peck-a-boo!

36

What is a ghost's favorite ride?
The roller ghoster!

What is a ghost's favorite game?
Hide and shriek!

What's a ghost's favorite food?
Grave-y!

What's a ghost's favorite ice cream
flavor?
Boo-berry!

What did the mother ghoul say to her naughty daughter?
Ghost stand in the corner!

Why could the little ghost see right through his father?
Because he was trans-parent!

What is an Australian ghost's favorite dessert?
Boo-meringue pie!

Knock-Knocking on
Mrs. Jeepers' Door

The Bailey School Kids are afraid to knock, but you're sure to find these jokes a knockout!

Knock-knock.
Who's there?
Howie.
Howie who?
I'm fine. Howie you?

Knock-knock.
Who's there?
Liza.
Liza who?
Liza terrible things to tell!

Knock-knock.
Who's there?
Turner.
Turner who?
Turner the page for some more knock-knock jokes!

Knock-knock.
Who's there?
Eddie.
Eddie who?
Eddie body home?

Knock-knock.
Who's there?
Melody.
Melody who?
Melody we roll along.

Knock-knock.
Who's there?
Razor.
Razor who?
Razor hands! This is a stickup!

Knock-knock.
Who's there?
Ivan.
Ivan who?
Ivan to suck your blood.

Knock-knock.
Who's there?
Eileen.
Eileen who?
Eileen over to tie my shoes.

Knock-knock.
Who's there?
Boo.
Boo who?
Please don't cry. It was only a joke.

You'll get all wrapped up in these silly jokes!

Coach Tuttle *from*
MUMMIES DON'T COACH SOFTBALL

Do mummies ever get presents?
Yes. On Mummies Day!

What is covered in bandages and has a
big bow around its neck?
A gift-wrapped mummy!

What room in a haunted house makes a
mummy nervous?
The living room.

What do mummies talk about when
they get together?
Old times!

What is a mummy after it is 2000 years old?
Two thousand and one.

How do mummies like their eggs?
Terri-*fried!*

How can you tell spaghetti from a mummy?
The mummy won't slip off the end of your fork.

What's the difference between a mummy and a grape?
The grape is purple!

Why was King Tut buried in a pyramid?
Because he was dead!

What is a mummy's favorite dessert?
Peaches and scream!

What do you call pizza that is 2000 years old and found in a mummy's tomb?
Cold!

Cyclops jokes
for you and *eye!*

Dr. Polly *from*
CYCLOPS DOESN'T ROLLER-SKATE

Howie: Did you hear about the evil
cyclops?
Liza: Yeah. He was so mean, even his
echo is afraid to answer him back!

What do you get if you cross a cyclops
with a skunk?
A dirty look from the cyclops!

Eddie: Why did the baby cyclops have
so many holes in his head?
Melody: He was learning to eat with a
fork!

45

Did you hear about the very short cyclops movie?
Don't blink or you'll miss it!

Mrs. Jeepers: Where does a cyclops go
     after junior high?
Mr. Davis: High ghoul!

Eddie: Why did the two cyclopes have a
     fight?
Howie: They couldn't see eye to eye!

What is a cyclops' normal eyesight?
20.

The Top Five Songs on the Bailey School Cafeteria Juke Box

Yellow Submarine Sandwich

Yankee Noodle Dandy

The Star-Spangled Banana

It Had to Be Stew

You Can Fry, You Can Fry, You Can Fry!

Coach Graves' Favorite Sports Shots!

They're sure to score with you!

Why didn't the first baseman get to dance with Cinderella?
He missed the ball!

How do you serve food to quarter-backs?
In souper bowls!

Why was the chicken thrown out at first base?
He hit a fowl ball.

How are teachers like umpires?
They both penalize you for errors.

What has 22 legs and goes slurp, slurp, slurp?
A football team drinking ice cream sodas.

Why do bakers make good baseball pitchers?
They know how to beat batters.

How do you get a rest during track and field practice?
Sit down on one of the laps!

Which soccer player is never promoted?
The left back.

When is a basketball player like a baby?
When he dribbles.

What did the soccer ball say to the halfback?
I get a kick out of you.

What color is a cheerleader?
Yeller!

These jokes will make you scream!

Miss MacFarland *from*
MONSTERS DON'T SCUBA DIVE

Where's a monster's favorite place to scuba dive?
Lake Eerie!

Monster student: I just ate my substitute teacher.
Monster principal: Okay, now eat your vegetables!

What is a monster's favorite sport?
Baseball. They like the double-headers.

What is a monster's favorite breakfast?
Bacon and legs!

What do you do with a green monster?
Wait for him to ripen.

How do you get in touch with the Loch
Ness monster?
Drop her a line.

Monster #1: I'm sorry I lost my head.
Monster #2: Don't worry about it. You've
     got another one.

Howie: What's the difference between a
     lemon, a monster, and a bag of ce-
     ment?
Eddie: What?
Howie: You can squeeze a lemon but
     you can't squeeze a monster.
Eddie: What about the bag of cement?
Howie: I just threw that in to make it
     hard!

What do you get if you cross a monster
with a dog?
A neighborhood without any cats!

Did you hear the story about the monster that ate New York?
Never mind, you'll never swallow it!

Did you hear the joke about the 50-foot monster?
Never mind. It's over your head.

How do you say monster in Japanese?
Monster in Japanese.

How do you make a banana shake?
Take it to a monster movie!

What do you call a charming, well-mannered, handsome monster?
A failure!

What is a monster's favorite drink?
Ghoul-aid!

What do you do with a blue monster?
Cheer him up!

Hey, Bailey School: It's D.E.A.R. (Drop Everything And Read) Time!

More wacky books from the
Bailey City library!

My Days at the Rodeo
by Larry Yet

A Picnic on the Beach
by Sandy Egg

Baseball Is My Life
by Hedda Homer

A Visit to the North Pole
by I. M. Freezing

Rain Forest Animals
by Harry Ape

Wishes can come true and food can be funny!

Eugene *from*
GENIES DON'T RIDE BICYCLES

What's red and very dangerous?
Shark-infested raspberry Jell-O!

What's long, orange, and wears diapers?
A *baby carrot!*

Liza: There's a bug in my macaroni.
Howie: Don't worry. It won't survive
long in that stuff.

Knock-knock.
Who's there?
Candy.
Candy who?
Candy cafeteria sell some good food for a change?

Eddie: Hey! There's a bug in my food.

Cafeteria worker: Well, take him home. And remember, you're not supposed to bring your pets to school.

How does a hungry kid eat a hot dog?
With relish!

Eddie: There's no chicken in my chicken soup.

Mrs. Tilly: So what? You don't find a dog in a dog biscuit, do you?

How do you make a hamburger roll?
Take it to the top of a steep hill and give it a push!

What dessert costs the most money?
A dough-nut!

Which vegetables should not be allowed in the boxing ring?
Spinach. It could get creamed!

What's worse than finding a worm in your apple?
Finding half a worm!

Nurse Redding's First Aid Funnies

Nurse Redding *from*
MARTIANS DON'T TAKE TEMPERATURES

Liza: Are the school lunches healthy?
Nurse Redding: I've never heard one
    complain!

How long should a doctor practice
medicine?
Until he gets it right!

Howie: Nurse Redding, why is doing
    nothing so tiring?
Nurse Redding: Because you can't stop
    to rest

What disease is a vampire afraid of?
Tooth decay!

What do you do if you have water on the knee, water on the brain, and water on the wrist?
Turn off the shower.

Nurse Smedley: Your cough sounds better today.
Melody: It should, I practiced all night.

What do dancers get when they eat too much?
Ballet-aches.

Why did the house call the doctor?
It had window panes.

Howie: What did they find when they X-rayed Ben's brain?
Eddie: Nothing.

Liza: What do you say to a doctor who is a real quack?
Eddie: What's up . . . *duck!*

Where does a rabbit go to have an operation?
To the ether bunny!

What do you give a sick bird?
A first aid tweetment.

 **Trust us — these jokes are well put together!**

Frank *from*
FRANKENSTEIN DOESN'T PLANT PETUNIAS

What happens when Frankenstein's monster swims in the dead sea?
He gets wet.

When Frankenstein's monster ran for president, what was his slogan?
Volt for me!

What do you get when Frankenstein's monster walks through your garden?
Squash!

How do you talk to Frankenstein's monster?
Politely!

How can you tell if Frankenstein's monster is in your lunchbox?
The lid won't close.

Howie: Frankenstein's monster helped make our neighborhood more beautiful.
Melody: How did he do that?
Howie: He moved away!

What did Frankenstein's monster say to the scarecrow?
I can beat the stuffing out of you!

Liza: What do you get if you cross Frankenstein's monster and a werewolf?

Howie: I don't know, but I don't think I'd want to wait around to find out!

Melody: Did Dr. Frankenstein make his monster laugh?

Dr. Victor: Yes. In fact, he kept him in stitches!

Ben: What would you get if you crossed Frankenstein's monster with the Invisible Man?

Carey: I don't know what you'd call it, but it wouldn't be much to look at!

What did Frankenstein's monster say to his bride?
You're so electrocute!

What goes ha-ha-ha-ha-plop?
Frankenstein's monster laughing his head off!

These elf jokes are pretty well-gnome!

Hollis Bell *from*
ELVES DON'T WEAR HARD HATS

What do little elves learn in school?
The elf-abet.

What do you call a dozen elves?
Tw'elves.

Santa's elf #1: What use is a reindeer?
Santa's elf #2: To make the flowers
    grow, sweetie.

What did the teacher say to the elf who
wouldn't leave school?
*What's the matter? Don't you have a
gnome to go to?*

Bailey School Class Pets

These animal jokes will keep you roaring!

Where do you take a sick stallion?
To the horsepital!

Why do fish travel in schools?
They have a lot of class!

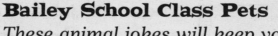

What do you call a crazy chicken?
A cuckoo cluck!

What kind of stories does a mother rabbit tell?
Hare-raising tales!

How is cat food sold?
It is priced purr can!

What is bad weather for mice and rats?
When it rains cats and dogs.

Why do hummingbirds hum?
They don't know the words!

What dog would you find at the
United Nations?
A diplomutt!

What did the duck say when it laid a
square egg?
Ouch!

What goes clomp clomp clomp
squish?
An elephant with one wet sneaker!

How are the tail of a dog and the
leaves of a tree alike?
*They are both pretty far from the
bark!*

Liza: Did you ever see a dogsled?
Melody: No, but I've seen a fishbowl.
Eddie: And I've seen a horsefly!

What do snakes do after a fight?
Hiss and make up!

What has two humps, is brown, and
lives at the North Pole?
A lost camel!

What kind of cars do cows drive?
Cattle-lacs!

These far-out jokes are a blast!

Mrs. Zork *from*
ALIENS DON'T WEAR BRACES

How do you get an alien baby to sleep?
You rocket!

How does an alien count to 20?
On one of its hands!

What do Martians have that no other creature has?
Baby Martians!

What does an alien do when he gets dirty?
He takes a meteor shower!

What is an alien's normal eyesight?
20-20-20-20!

Eddie: Imagine you were alone in a field, surrounded by aliens that wanted to capture you and bring you to their distant planet. What would you do?

Liza: I'd stop imagining!

Where do aliens leave their cars while they shop?
At a parking meteor!

What do you call cows that eat grass in space?
Star-grazers!

What is green and jumps three feet every ten seconds?
A Martian with hiccups!

How do Martian cowboys talk to each other?
They use communication saddle-lights!

Are You Afraid to Knock on the School Office Door?

Mrs. Kidwell *from*
GREMLINS DON'T CHEW BUBBLE GUM

Knock-knock.
Who's there?
Lena.
Lena who?
Lena little closer and I'll kiss you.

Knock-knock.
Who's there?
Banana.
Banana who?
Knock-knock.
Who's there?
Banana.
Banana who?
Knock-knock.
Who's there?

Banana.
Banana who?
Knock-knock.
Who's there?
Orange.
Orange who?
*Orange you glad I didn't say banana
again?*

Knock-knock.
Who's there?
Arthur.
Arthur who?
*Arthur any more knock-knock jokes
coming my way?*

Knock knock.
Who's there?
Willis.
Willis who?
Willis knock knock joking ever stop?

Bailey School's Out for Summer!

Captain Teach *from*
PIRATES DON'T WEAR PINK SUNGLASSES

What is grey and has four legs and a trunk?
A mouse going on vacation!

Liza: How did you find the weather at
camp?
Melody: Simple. I went outside and
there it was!

What do you call a person who thinks
he has wings and can fly?
Plane crazy?

How did the comedian travel during his vacation?
In his jokeswagon!

Why didn't the leopard go away on her vacation? .
She just couldn't find the right spot!